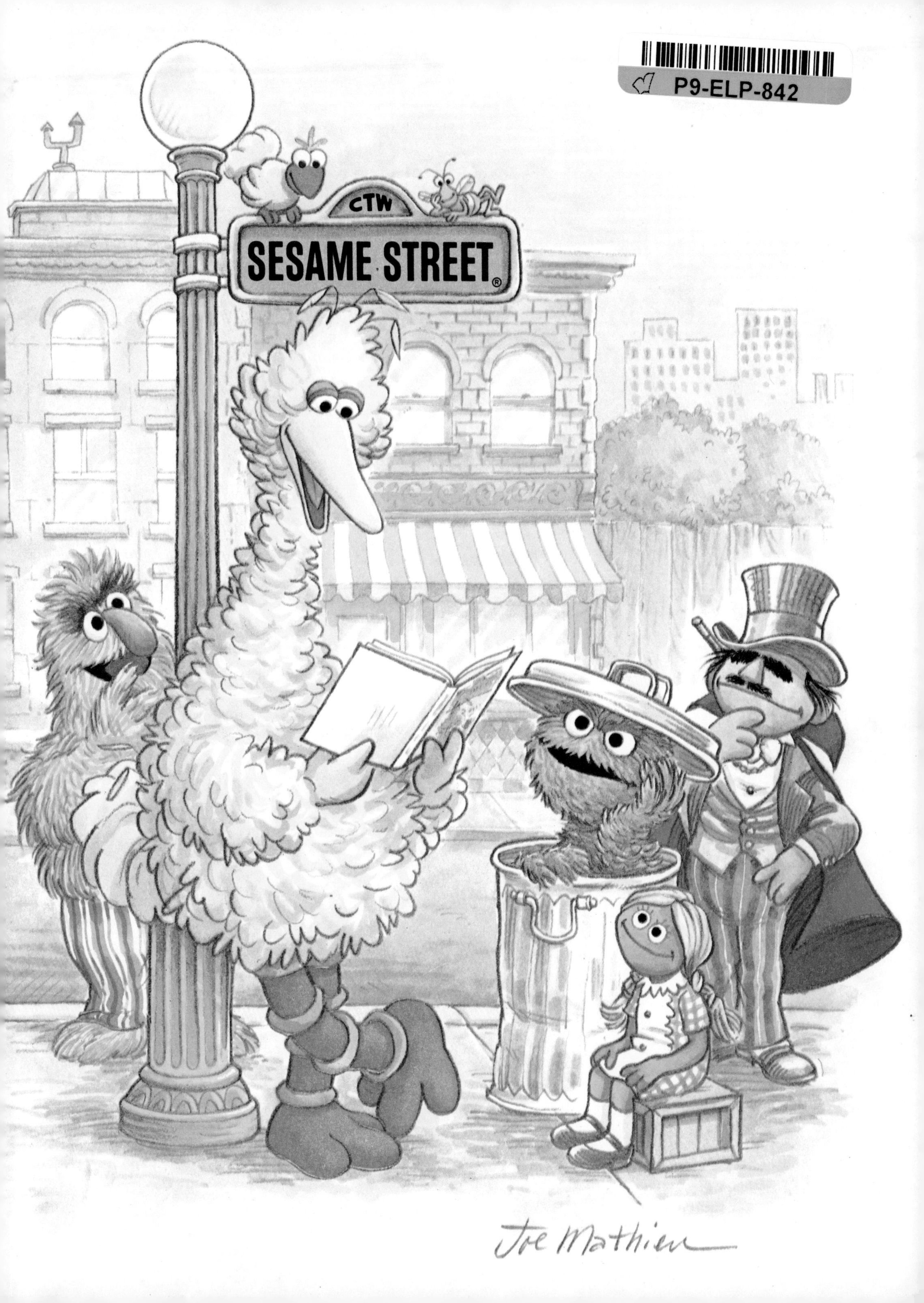
P9-ELP-842
CTW
SESAME STREET®
Joe Mathieu

VOLUME 1

FEATURING
THE LETTERS
A AND B
AND THE NUMBER
1

Children's Television Workshop/Funk & Wagnalls, Inc.

WRITTEN BY:
Michael Frith
Jerry Juhl
Emily Perl Kingsley
Sharon Lerner
Nina B. Link
Albert G. Miller
Jeffrey Moss
Norman Stiles
Jon Stone
Daniel Wilcox

ILLUSTRATED BY:
Mel Crawford
Michael Frith
Joseph Mathieu
Harry McNaught
Kelly Oechsli
Michael J. Smollin
Caroll Spinney

PHOTOGRAPHS BY:
Charles P. Rowan

 Published in the United States by Random House, Inc., New York, and simultaneously in Canada by Random House of Canada Limited, Toronto, in conjunction with the Children's Television Workshop. Distributed by Funk & Wagnalls, Inc., New York, N.Y. Manufactured in the United States of America.

0-8343-0009-5

1 2 3 4 5 6 7 8 9 0

A
a A
An A Story
Once upon a time,
in a far-away kingdom,
there lived a queen
named Queen Agatha.
One day, Queen Agatha
called all the knights
of the kingdom
to the throne room.
I love things that begin with A!
A
J. Mathieu

"Knights of the kingdom," announced Queen Agatha, "I love things that begin with A. Whoever can bring me something that begins with the letter A will be rewarded handsomely. *Perhaps* the winner will dance with me at the royal party tonight."

"Oh, boy!" said Sir Bird. "I'm heading for the Royal Zoo! That's the only place where I can find something that begins with the letter A. I'll be right back, Queen Agatha!"

Sir Bird hurried from the throne room, pausing only long enough to take an apple from a bowl near the throne room door.

"I'd better bring this apple with me," he said, "in case I get hungry on my way to the zoo."

Once outside the castle, Sir Bird realized that he was lost.

"Oh, no, I'm lost!" cried Sir Bird. "If only there were something to help me find my way to the Royal Zoo."

Just then, Sir Bird passed a large arrow. The arrow said, "This way to the zoo."

"Oh, look at that arrow!" exclaimed Sir Bird. "That arrow will help me find my way."

So he grabbed the arrow and followed it until he reached his destination—a cage in the Royal Zoo where there sat a happy-looking alligator.

"Oh, Mr. Alligator, I've found you at last," said Sir Bird. "Your name begins with the letter A. Won't you please come with me, back to the throne room?"

Since the alligator had never before seen a throne room, he was more than happy to follow Sir Bird.

When he reached the throne room,
Sir Bird announced to the Queen,
"Queen Agatha, this alligator's name begins with the letter A. I guess now I can dance with you at the royal party, huh?"

"Well," said the Queen,
"first of all that apple and that arrow you have also begin with the letter A."

"Oh, how silly of me!" said Sir Bird. "I grabbed the apple and the arrow without realizing that they began with the letter A. But I guess that since I brought you an apple and an arrow and an alligator, I can dance with you at the royal party for sure."

"Well...if it's all the same to you, I'd like to dance with your friend! You're a pretty handsome guy, you know that?" said the Queen to the alligator.

Then she said to Sir Bird, "Sir Bird, since you found the letter A, I will give you a lifetime supply of birdseed. And, I will make you my Ambassador to Antarctica."

"Oh, boy!" said Sir Bird. And Sir Bird was very happy. And so was the Queen. As for the alligator, he was happy, too, because he had always wanted to dance with a Queen. And since everybody is happy, the story is over.

howdy! It is I, the Count. I am riding a wild bucking bronco horsey. But not only can I ride him...I can COUNT him, too! 1! One horsey! Ha, ha, ha.
1
J. Mathieu

Cookie Monster's Famous Cookie Dough

Dear Reader,

Hello, there! Me COOKIE MONSTER and my favorite thing is EATING COOKIES.

In this wonderful set of books me going to show you how to make ALL KINDS OF COOKIES! But first . . . me tell you secret recipe for

COOKIE DOUGH (It been in my family for years.)

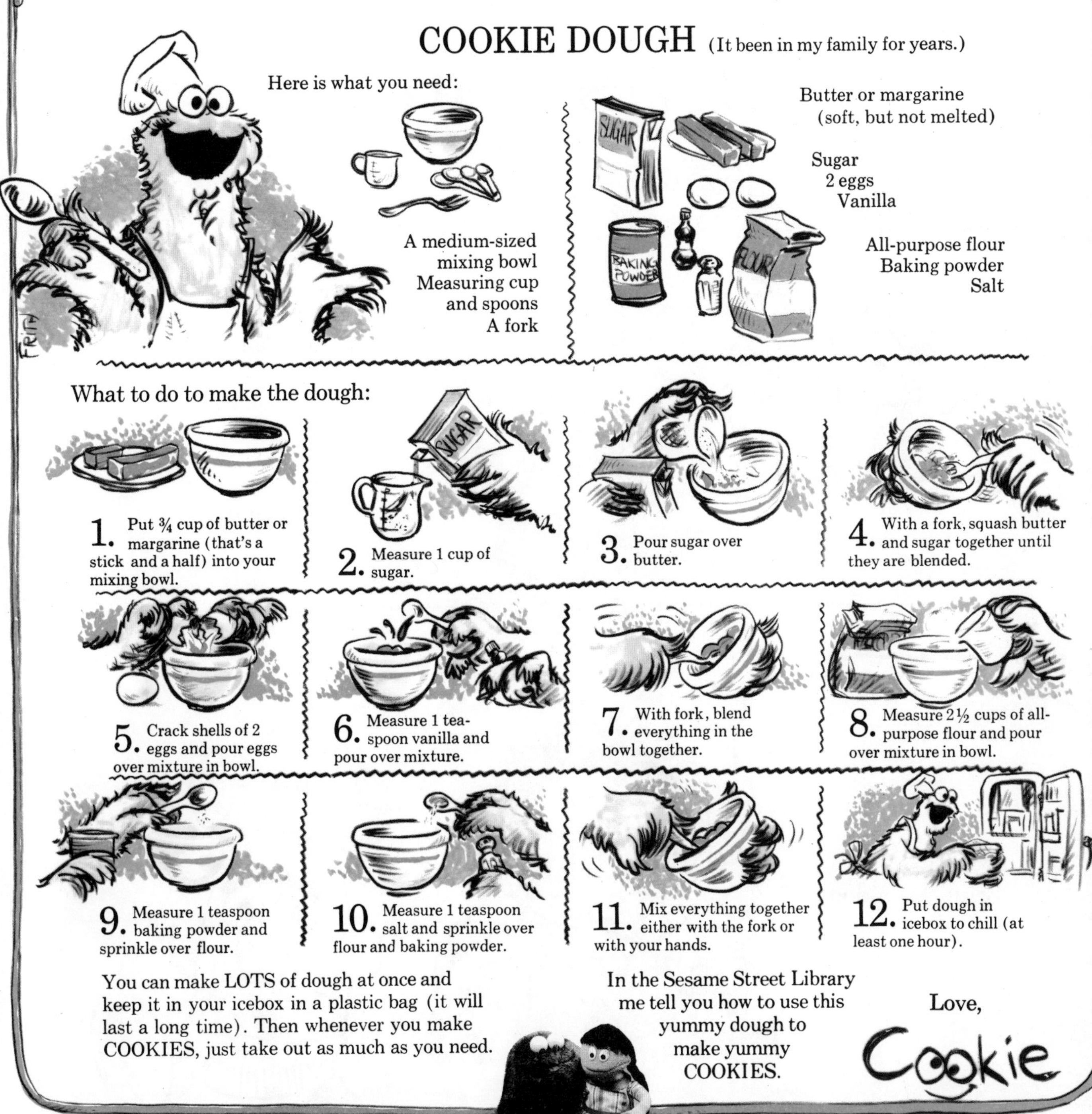

Here is what you need:

A medium-sized mixing bowl
Measuring cup and spoons
A fork

Butter or margarine (soft, but not melted)
Sugar
2 eggs
Vanilla
All-purpose flour
Baking powder
Salt

What to do to make the dough:

1. Put ¾ cup of butter or margarine (that's a stick and a half) into your mixing bowl.
2. Measure 1 cup of sugar.
3. Pour sugar over butter.
4. With a fork, squash butter and sugar together until they are blended.
5. Crack shells of 2 eggs and pour eggs over mixture in bowl.
6. Measure 1 teaspoon vanilla and pour over mixture.
7. With fork, blend everything in the bowl together.
8. Measure 2½ cups of all-purpose flour and pour over mixture in bowl.
9. Measure 1 teaspoon baking powder and sprinkle over flour.
10. Measure 1 teaspoon salt and sprinkle over flour and baking powder.
11. Mix everything together either with the fork or with your hands.
12. Put dough in icebox to chill (at least one hour).

You can make LOTS of dough at once and keep it in your icebox in a plastic bag (it will last a long time). Then whenever you make COOKIES, just take out as much as you need.

In the Sesame Street Library me tell you how to use this yummy dough to make yummy COOKIES.

Love,

Cookie

1

Bert's Bath

"Hey, Bert," said Ernie one bright sunny day. "Let's go out and play some football."

"Ernie, I can't go play football," said Bert. "Can't you see I'm going to take a bath now? I can't play football."

"Gee, Bert," said Ernie, "you don't have everything you need to take a bath. You need **1** more thing."

"Oh?" said Bert. "I do?"

"Yes!" said Ernie. "You need **1 rubber duckie** to keep you company. Here it is."

"O.K., Ernie," Bert said. "Thanks a lot. Now I'm going to take my bath."

"Wait a second, Bert," Ernie said. "I forgot. You'll need **1** more thing in your bath. You might get hungry, so here is **1 sandwich** for you to eat."

"A sandwich?" cried Bert. "How can I eat a sandwich in the bathtub?"

"You're right," said Ernie. "You'll need **1** more thing. You don't want to get crumbs in the tubby...so you will need **1 table** to eat your sandwich on."

"Come on, Ernie," groaned Bert. "I can't take a bath with all that stuff."

"Of course you can't!" said Ernie. "You need **1** more thing. You need to have some nice music to listen to. You need **1 piano**."

"Ernie!" yelled Bert. "This is ridiculous. I can't play the piano while I take a bath!"

"You certainly can't," Ernie said. "How silly of me. Just **1** more thing and then everything will be ready."

"There you are," said Ernie. "**1 elephant** to play the piano for you.

"Ernie!" shouted Bert. "Will you look at this! With your **just 1 more thing,** and **1 more thing,** you've filled up the whole bathtub and there's no room for me in there! Now I can't take a bath at all!"

"In that case," said Ernie, "how about going out to play a little football with me, huh, Bert?"

ERNIE PRESENTS THE LETTER A
Now it's time to study the letter A. One word that begins with A is APPLE.
A
This is an APPLE. Do you know what to do with an APPLE?
You eat it. Ha-ha.

A Happy-Sad-Happy Sad-Happy Story

I have a story for you. It's about being HAPPY and being SAD. You can help me with your HAPPY—SAD masks. Whenever the people in the story are happy, hold up your HAPPY face mask and shout YAY! And when the story is sad, show the SAD side and say BOO-HOO! O.K., are you ready?

Once upon a time, in a little house near a little forest, there lived a little girl and a little boy. And they were very HAPPY.

But, one day, when the little boy went to the icebox to get something for lunch, all he could find was some liverwurst—and they both HATED liverwurst. And that made them very SAD.

"I have an idea," said the little girl. "Let's make liverwurst sandwiches and have a picnic. That will be fun!" And that idea made them very HAPPY.

So off they went into the forest to have their picnic. But no sooner had they spread out their picnic blanket, than a MONSTER jumped out from behind the trees. "LIVERWURST!" he yelled, and gobbled up all their sandwiches. This made the children very SAD.

BOO HOO!

When the monster saw how sad they were he reached into his pocket and pulled out a bag full of peanut butter and jelly sandwiches. "Here," he said. "My mommy made me peanut butter and jelly sandwiches for lunch and me HATE peanut butter and jelly. Me was so SAD until me saw your liverwurst. But that make me very HAPPY!"

FRITH

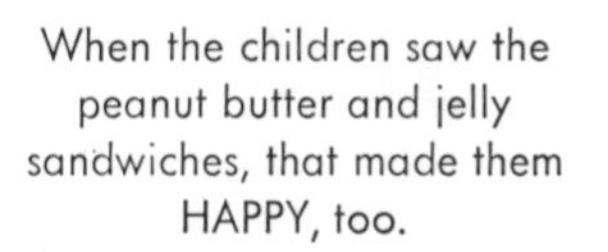

When the children saw the peanut butter and jelly sandwiches, that made them HAPPY, too.

YAY!

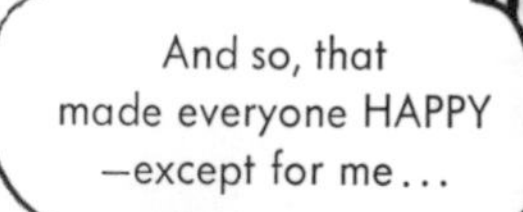

And so, that made everyone HAPPY —except for me...

...because this is the end of the story— and that makes *me* SAD.

HOW TO MAKE A HAPPY-SAD MASK:

Just take a paper plate or a round piece of cardboard.

On one side draw a HAPPY face...

...On the other side draw a SAD face.

Take a paper towel tube and make a slit in the top. Then slip in your HAPPY—SAD face...and that's it.

Now are you HAPPY?

Herry Monster, Policeman

Big Bird, Mail Carrier

THE PRINCESS AND THE COOKIE

In a castle on a mountain
There was once a friendly King,
And he would have been quite happy
But for one annoying thing;
What upset him was a problem
That disturbed him night and day:
It was how to find a husband
For his daughter Princess Kay.

"I am tiny," said the Princess,
"Very delicate and sweet.
I will marry any fellow
Who can bake my best-loved treat.
Do you know what that is, Daddy?
Do you know my favorite thing?
Do you know what I'm so hooked on?"
"Sure, it's COOKIES!" said the King.

"Yes, my greatest treat is COOKIES,"
Said the Princess with a sigh,
"But they must be small and dainty,
And as delicate as I.
If a man who baked such cookies
Came to visit me," said Kay,
"I would fall in love that *minute.*
I would marry him that day!"

Said the King, "A dozen princes
Have brought cookies here to taste.
But the trouble that they went to—
It was just a total waste!
When you taste their sample cookies
You've but one rude word to say.
Can you tell me what the word is?"
"Sure, it's 'BLECCH'," said Princess Kay.

"That is right," her dad continued,
"And it pains my royal neck
When you nibble on a cookie,
Hold your nose, and holler 'BLECCH!'
You are mighty picky, daughter!
I can *not* believe it's true
That those princes' homemade cookies
Were not good enough for you."

"Bring a fellow," said the Princess,
"With a cookie in his paw
That is tiny and delicious,
And you'll have a son-in-law."
Said her dad, "Three handsome princes
Have arrived from distant lands.
They are waiting in the parlor,
Holding cookies in their hands."

In the castle's royal parlor
Stood a prince in uniform.
"Here's a cookie, dear," he whispered,
"Better eat it while it's warm."
Said the King, "Boy, that's so tiny,
It's no bigger than a speck.
What's the word for this one, daughter?"
Said the royal Princess: "BLECCH!"

Then the prince said, "You're bananas!"
Stamped his foot upon the floor,
Threw the cookie on the table
And went marching out the door.
"*He's* bananas," said the Princess,
"That one will not do at all!
That cookie is not *tiny* . . .
I would say it's only . . . small!"

When the second prince was summoned,
In he pranced in shining armor.
"Take this cookie, babe," he murmured,
"I just baked it—it's a charmer."

"That's just *your* opinion, Charlie,"
Said the Princess with a pout.
"Leave your cookie on the table
And my maid will show you out."

When the third prince made his entrance,
He was treated just the same,
And he left the royal castle
Just as quickly as he came.

Then the King said, "Well, dear daughter,
You have made your dad a wreck.
You will never find a husband
'Cause you're always saying 'BLECCH!'"

Just about a minute later,
From the castle kitchen wing,
There appeared the Cookie Monster,
Private baker to the King.
In his hand the baker carried,
On a teeny-weeny tray,
One delicious-looking cookie—
Small and delicate as Kay.

"Made this cookie," said the Monster,
"Smallest one you'll ever meet.
Well, so long, old King and Princess,
Gonna take outside and eat."
"*Hold that cookie!*" cried the Princess,
"It's the one I long for. WOW!
Let me eat your perfect cookie
And I'll marry you right now."

"Nothin' doin'!" said the Monster,
"Cookie made for me alone!"
"But," the King said, "give it to her
And you'll sit upon a throne!
Give that cookie to my daughter
And who knows how far you'll go.
You'll no longer be a baker,
But a *prince* with lots of dough."

"No! No! No!" exclaimed the Monster.
But then, looking down, he saw
Three more cookies that were lying
On the table near his paw.
"Cookies!" bellowed Cookie Monster,
"Great *big* cookies! Son-of-gun!"
Cried the King, "Then trade them! Trade them!
Give my Kay your tiny one!"

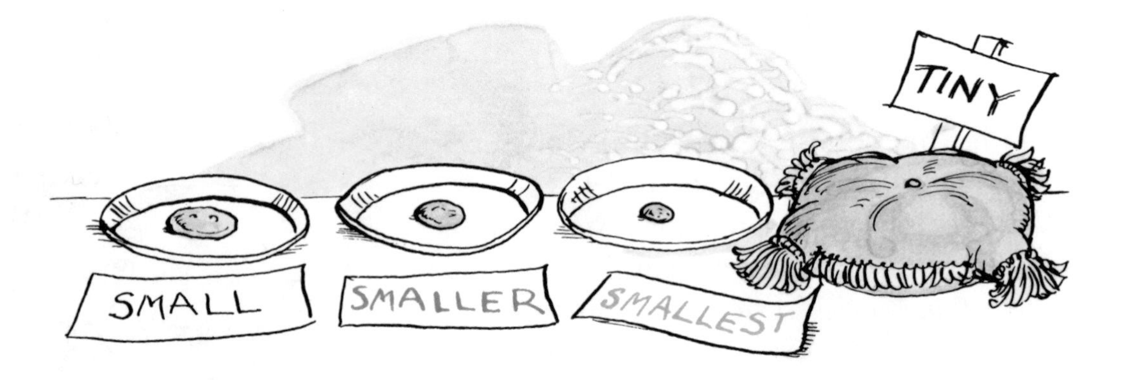

"Oh boy!" said the Cookie Monster,
"It's a deal—I eat these three!
Princess Kay can eat *my* cookie,
But no have to marry me."
"But you MUST!" the King commanded,
Hugging him around the neck,
"Welcome to the family, baker."
Said the Cookie Monster: "BLECCH!"

1 2 3 4 5 6 7

Oh my goodness,
you are a very
big bird!

Cookie Monster's Shape Cookies
Salutations! (That mean "Hi, there!")
Me back for DELICIOUS page of COOKIE making. This time me show you how to make different- SHAPED cookies. O.K.? This one pretty tricky.
First, take some cookie dough out of icebox. If you all *out* of cookie dough (oh dear!) just make some more!
Sprinkle cloth with flour and put dough on cloth. Roll dough out flat, about 1/4 inch thick. Now come the tricky part—need to find things to make SHAPES with. Let me see . . . Ah! Can use GLASS to make round cookies . . . and those box lids make good rectangles and squares.
Me just push them down on dough and peel away dough on outside.
First me make circles . . .
Then me make squares and rectangles.
But how me make triangle?
Aha! Good idea! Me cut square in half, like this!
Me make TWO triangles.
Now me heat oven to 400 degrees, put cookies on ungreased cookie sheet, and put cookie sheet in oven. O.K., now come hard part again. Me have to wait six to eight minutes while cookies cook. What me going to eat? Furniture all gone. . . .
Wait a minute! Did me say PAGE was delicious? Me try—YUM . . . pretty good. (It nice rectangle, too.)
Remember: More delicious cookies coming in Volume 2.
FRITH

Bert and the Beanstalk

Once upon a time, there lived a boy named Bert. One day Bert traded the family bicycle for a bag of magic beans.

But Bert's buddy, Ernie, looked in the bag and said, "Beans? Blah! How boring." And he threw the boring beans out the back window.

Immediately, the beans began to bloom. By breakfast, they had blossomed into a big, beautiful beanstalk.

When Ernie saw the beanstalk he said, "Look. A big, beautiful beanstalk. That's *really* boring."

But Bert wasn't a bit bored. "I feel brave!" Bert bellowed. So he bounded up the beanstalk.

Up, up, up went Bert, beyond the bean blossoms, beyond the birds, beyond the blue . . . until he came to a big black building.

The building belonged to a giant named Burly Barney. Burly Barney was in the bedroom eating his breakfast of bushels of buttered buns, barrels of blueberries and bunches of bananas. When Bert saw how big Burly Barney was, Bert beat it to the back room.

There, Bert found a big basket. It was full of bottlecaps.

"Boy, oh boy, oh boy!" said Bert. "Bottlecaps! I collect bottlecaps!" So Bert brought the basket of bottlecaps back to the beanstalk.

But Burly Barney saw Bert, and he began to bellow, "You took my bottlecaps!" "I'd better beat it," said Bert.

Boldly, Bert climbed down. Barney bounded down behind him. But, on a bottom branch, Bert slipped and fell with a bump.

"I'll bet you want to bash me because I borrowed your basket of bottlecaps," blurted Bert.

"Are you batty?" bellowed Burly Barney. "Those bottlecaps are boring! They were driving me bananas! Thank you for borrowing my bottlecaps!"

And Burly Barney shook Bert's hand. In fact, he shook Bert's whole body. Then Barney bounded back up the beanstalk to his beautiful black building.

And now that the basket of bottlecaps belonged to Bert, Bert had the best and biggest bunch of bottlecaps on the block. So Bert was beaming.

And everyone lived blissfully ever after. Except Ernie . . . who was bored.

Oh, brother— that's BORING!

Ernie and Bert Present...
Shape Pictures
Ernie,
I have the square,
the triangle, and
the rectangle. All
you had to get
was the circle.
?
How can we
make shape pictures
if you don't have
the circle?
Bert and Ernie
are proud to present
SHAPE PICTURES!
Here are some
pictures we made out of these
shapes... And here are some extra
shapes for YOU to make
pictures out of. That triangle
might make a *nifty* pigeon...
Hey, Berd... cad I hab
by dose bag dow?

Oscar's Worst Day

This is a picture of ME, Oscar the Grouch. And this is the day I hate most. Everybody is getting ready to CLEAN UP Sesame Street.

It's awful. They sweep all the nice dirt off the sidewalks. They pick up all the wonderful, yucchy trash that's lying around. They get rid of all the old tin cans and papers on the street. Then do you know where they put all that stuff...

IN THE TRASH CANS! You know, some things about Clean-Up Day aren't so bad... if you happen to live in a trash can, that is.

The Princess and the Pea

One dark and stormy night a girl knocked at the door of a royal palace.

"I am a princess," she said. "I got lost in the storm and my horse ran away. Will you let me stay the night?"

"A princess indeed!" said the queen. The girl's clothes were torn and muddy and her hair was a mess. But when the prince saw the girl's lovely smile, he begged his mother to let her stay.

As soon as the queen noticed that the prince was interested in the girl, she decided she must find out if the stranger was a *real* princess. So she put a pea upon a mattress and piled 12 *more* mattresses on top. Then she gave the girl a ladder and told her to sleep well.

The queen hurried to tell the prince about her plan. "If she feels that tiny pea, she's got to be a *real* princess," said the queen.

The next morning the girl came out of her room looking very tired. "I couldn't sleep at all," she moaned. "There was a lump in my mattress."

"She *is* a real princess!" gasped the queen.

"Even if she isn't, I love her anyway," said the prince happily. And when he asked the princess to be his bride, she said yes.

Does Ernie draw
with his left
or right hand?

He
draws
with a
crayon!

Crafts for All Seasons

Spring

Hello, everybodee! This is Old Farmer Grover here. It is springtime, and spring is the time when all the pretty flowers bloom. I will show you how to make some flowers of your own.

Get some paper cups, some straws, some paste, and some paper and crayons. Draw some BEAUTIFUL flowers on the paper, cut them out, and stick them to the straws. Then put some sand in the cups and stick the straws in the sand. AREN'T THEY BEAUTIFUL?

You can even decorate the cups, like I did.

Summer

You know what us Grouches like to do in the summer? We like to go down to the *swamp* and play in the MUD. Here are some of my favorite MUD toys...

The best thing to use is a plastic bleach bottle. You can cut off the bottom, and use it for a pail.

And you can cut the top, like this... and it makes a super-dooper *mud* scooper.

Of course, if you're not a grouch you can use them at the beach for SAND toys...

...BLECCH!

KNEE DEEP!

Fall

Hi, I'm Betty Lou. When the fall winds blow, I love to make pretty pinwheels and watch them spin. First, take a square piece of paper and color it with bright designs on both sides.

Then fold it in half, like this...

and then again, like this...

Now draw a small circle right in the middle of the paper. Cut on the fold lines toward the middle, until you reach the outside of your circle. BE SURE you don't cut all the way through the middle.

Now take one corner of each triangle and stick it to your middle circle like this...

Last of all, take a pin and a straw, and stick the pin through the middle of the pinwheel and through the straw.

(Stick a piece of cork or the eraser from a pencil on the pin so you won't get pricked.)

Now you can take your pinwheel out for a spin.

Winter

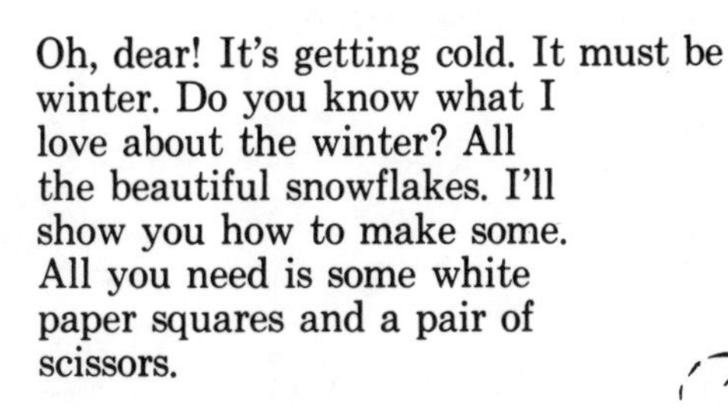

Oh, dear! It's getting cold. It must be winter. Do you know what I love about the winter? All the beautiful snowflakes. I'll show you how to make some. All you need is some white paper squares and a pair of scissors.

First fold your paper in half.
Then fold it in half again...
and then fold it one MORE time, into a triangle.

Now snip out bits from each side of the triangle.

Be sure to leave some space between each snip.

You can make all different kinds of snowflakes to hang on your walls and windows. Isn't that nice?

Hey, Bert. This was a great book, wasn't it?
Ernie

It sure was, Ernie. But wait till you see Volume 2.
Bert